◇▽◇▽◇▽◇▽◇▽◇▽◇

Leo's world is full of **MONSTERS**, but his family, friends, and fellow villagers know nothing about that. What lies beyond the Village Wall is **TOP SECRET** and, as the **GUARDIAN'S APPRENTICE**, Leo has sworn to keep this secret safe.

Armed with a **SLINGSHOT**, pouch of **MAGICAL STONES**, and **MONSTER MAP**, it's Leo's job to keep his world in balance—protecting his village from the monsters that surround it.

◇▽◇▽◇▽◇▽◇

OXFORD
UNIVERSITY PRESS

Great Clarendon Street, Oxford OX2 6DP

Oxford University Press is a department of the University of Oxford.
It furthers the University's objective of excellence in research, scholarship,
and education by publishing worldwide. Oxford is a registered trade mark of
Oxford University Press in the UK and in certain other countries

Text copyright © Kris Humphrey 2021
Illustrations copyright © Pete Williamson 2021

The moral rights of the author have been asserted

First published 2021

Database right Oxford University Press (maker)

British Library Cataloguing in Publication Data
Data available

ISBN: 978-0-19-277482-8

1 3 5 7 9 10 8 6 4 2

Printed in India

Paper used in the production of this book is a natural,
recyclable product made from wood grown in sustainable forests.
The manufacturing process conforms to the environmental
regulations of the country of origin.

LEO'S MAP OF MONSTERS

THE SPITFANG LIZARD

KRIS HUMPHREY

ILLUSTRATED BY
PETE WILLIAMSON

OXFORD
UNIVERSITY PRESS

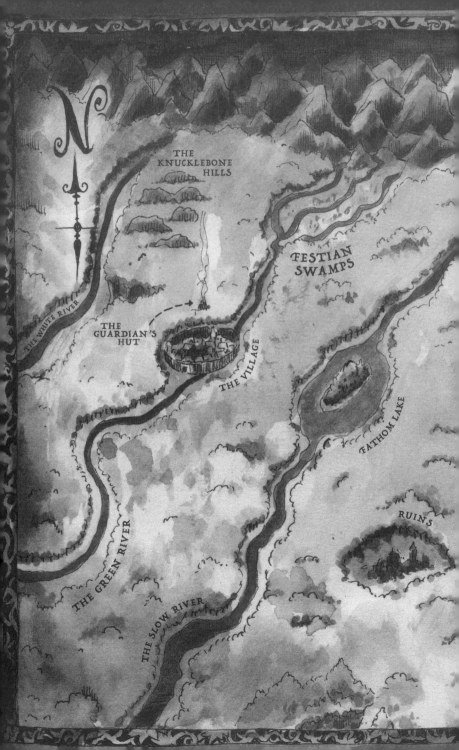

MEET THE CHARACTERS

LEO: THE GUARDIAN'S APPRENTICE

GILDA: THE TOWN CHIEF

HENRIK: THE GUARDIAN

STARLA: LEO'S MONSTER FRIEND

JACOB: LEO'S BEST FRIEND

ONe

A cold wind raced through the forest, shaking the trees and pelting me with dead autumn leaves. I crept through the undergrowth with my slingshot loaded and ready, scanning the treetops and listening hard for any sign of movement.

Somewhere close by there was a Treeshark, a monster so rare and deadly that even Henrik had seemed afraid when he'd spoken its name. Apparently, Treesharks hibernated for ten or twelve years at a time, high up near the mountains, but when they woke they liked nothing better than to set out on a week-long feeding frenzy down in the forest.

A crashing noise behind me made me turn, my slingshot raised and my heart pounding. I stared into the canopy, straining to spot the hulking, irregular shadow Henrik had warned me about.

But there was no shadow, just a large branch clattering its way towards the forest floor, torn from its trunk by the wind.

I continued on my way, creeping
deeper and deeper into the forest.

A few minutes later, at the base of a
shallow slope, I paused.

There was something up ahead.

I peered through the trembling branches, up the slope and into the canopy of one of the taller yew trees. There was a shadow: large, many-limbed, and deathly still between the boughs of the tree.

I swallowed hard and raised my slingshot.

The monster was twenty paces away. I could try for the shot now, but there were so many branches in the way, there would be no point. I needed to get closer.

But just as I started moving, the shadow in the yew tree lurched into action.

It crashed towards me, smashing branches aside as if they were nothing.

I held steady and aimed. The stone in my hand was cold and the tension in the slingshot pulled at the muscles in my forearm.

The Treeshark was almost on me now, this was my chance.

I fired my stone and watched it crack into the right side of the beast.

Then I leaped aside, rolling onto the ground as the huge shape swept past.

I jumped to my feet and watched the Treeshark crash into the trees beyond. Gradually, it slowed and changed direction, moving towards me again.

But I didn't load my slingshot this time. Instead I just stood aside as it swung back and forth, slowing down then finally coming to a standstill.

'Not bad, eh?' I shouted, reaching up and poking the Treeshark-shaped bundle of sticks and sacking so it swung a bit more on its rope.

'Henrik?'

I looked around, but there was no sign of the Guardian.

'You missed,' Henrik grunted, appearing alarmingly close behind me.

'What do you mean?' I said. 'I hit it! On the right side. You must have heard it?'

'Oh, I heard it, lad,' Henrik said. 'And I saw it. A glancing blow, that's all. Not good enough for a *real* Treeshark.'

'Yeah, but . . .'

'But nothing,' Henrik cut in. 'A flood-stone directly into the mouth is the only way to stop a hungry Treeshark. It's the only shark in the world that can't stand water.' He inspected the fake monster.

'You barely scraped a hit, boy. By now you'd be shark food. You know that.'

Technically, he was right, but I was still counting it as a hit.

'Let's go,' Henrik said, leading me back towards the cabin. 'Looks likc you need some more time with the books.'

I'd spent most of the last three weeks with the books: *Vanguard's Bestiary*, *Forest Creatures* by Rufus Wrangler, *The Budget Compendium of All-Devouring Terrors* by Hugo Beed. I was getting good at that part of the job, and I quite enjoyed it, too—learning the names and habits of the monsters, studying the Map of Monsters and learning how to use it—I'd even figured out how to tell most of the slingshot stones apart.

The problem, obviously, was my aim. I'd spent countless hours practising, and according to Henrik all I'd managed was 'a very slight improvement'.

We reached the cabin and I left the slingshot and Map on Henrik's desk.

'Don't be late back,' the Guardian growled at me as I headed for the door. 'We don't have time for one of these extra-long lunch breaks you seem to enjoy.'

'I'll be as quick as I can,' I replied, grumpily shoving my way out into the forest. If I tried to eat lunch any faster, I'd have to stop chewing all together.

I hurried through the thorn thicket and turned right at the pointed stone that marked the way to the village. A few moments later I was striding into the shadow of the Village Wall, my hand outstretched to feel for the secret door.

'Leo! Hey!'

I swung around at the sound of my name.

For a moment I thought it was Starla. I hadn't seen her for weeks, and I was worried she might have left the forest completely. But when I looked up I saw Jacob, ten paces above me, leaning over the Wall's high parapet.

'You want to eat lunch together?' he called, grinning.

I grinned back at him.

'You're not supposed to be up there!' I said.

Jacob shrugged.

'It's the only way I can get hold of you these days,' he said.

'Meet me at the bakery,' I shouted, heading towards the East Gate.

The monsters were a secret, and so was my Assignment as an apprentice Guardian. If anyone found out then villagers and monsters could both get hurt. I'd told Jacob and everyone else that my Assignment was 'forest maintenance', so they knew I left the village each day. But I still had to make sure no one saw where I went. That's why I used the secret door. But now Jacob had seen me I'd have to be more careful.

I made it to the bakery just before Jacob did, and we were soon winding our way through the bustling village streets.

'You should have seen Master Aldred's tunic today,' Jacob said. 'He'd basically spilled his entire breakfast down it. Like he hadn't even tried to get it in his mouth.'

I laughed.

The Record Keeper was messy, that

was true, but he'd always been kind to Jacob and me, letting us hang around in the Records Office, lending us books and giving us paper to draw on if we wanted it. A part of me still wondered whether I should have joined Jacob on Assignment there when Gilda had given me the choice. But it was too late now. I was an Apprentice Guardian and it was my responsibility to keep the village and the monsters safe.

When we arrived at my house, Mum was there to greet us.

'Afternoon, boys,' she said, smiling as she looked up from a large sheet of parchment covered in scribbled words and diagrams. She was helping to plan the midwinter festival this year. 'You can help yourselves to lunch today,' she said, nodding towards the table where the remnants of her own lunch were still out: apples and cheese, a long golden-brown loaf, and a small pot of fresh butter.

'Thanks,' Jacob said, tucking in straight away.

I shared a smile with Mum then grabbed an apple, only to be interrupted by an urgent burst of knocking at the door.

I looked round and saw Mum frowning down at her work. Beside me, Jacob munched on obliviously.

'Will you get that, Leo?' Mum asked.

I took a bite of my apple and went to the door, opening it just as another round of knocking began.

First, I saw a raised fist. Then, as the visitor lowered their arm, I found myself confronted by a red-faced, slightly angry-looking girl I recognized as Astrid the village messenger.

'Thanks for bothering to answer the door,' Astrid said, panting heavily. 'Message from . . .'

She paused for breath, doubling over with her hands on her knees. When she straightened up she didn't look much better.

'Message from the Village Chief,' she blurted out quickly before taking another deep breath. 'The turnip man requests your assistance,' she said. Then a frown and another deep breath. 'Apparently.'

I felt a shiver of excitement and trepidation. 'Turnip' was Gilda's code word. It meant I was needed in the forest immediately. I swallowed my mouthful of apple, thanked Astrid and closed the door on her.

'I have to go,' I said.

Mum and Jacob both stared at me, puzzled.

'The turnip man?' Jacob said.

I nodded, trying to come up with

something believable.

'Mouldy turnips,' I said, immediately regretting it. 'I get rid of them for him. Chuck them into the forest.'

I looked from Jacob to Mum. They seemed even more puzzled now.

'He gets angry if I'm late,' I said, shrugging.

Mum stared at me for a moment, then her face grew serious.

'Well, don't let him be mean to you,' she said. 'Or he'll have me to answer to.'

'I won't,' I said, heading towards the door and worrying that I'd got an innocent turnip man into trouble.

I rushed through the back streets of

the village and soon reached the turnip man's house. He was still fast asleep on his stool, surrounded by turnips. I strode past him, not bothering to be quiet, and a few moments later I was closing the secret door behind me and stepping out into the wind-shaken trees.

If Henrik had called for me, it meant a monster was near—a real one. I felt a nervous twist in my stomach. Maybe Henrik would come with me this time? His leg was almost healed, after all.

I made my way back through the thorn thicket and as I approached the cabin I heard voices. Gilda, the Village Chief, was inside and she seemed to be arguing with Henrik. I was about to go inside when I heard my name spoken, causing me to stop on the doorstep and listen.

'But Leo's so young,' Gilda said. 'What if something happens to him?'

'There's no use mollycoddling the boy,' Henrik replied. 'He's got to learn his trade.'

'And what if he gets eaten?' the Village Chief went on. 'What would I tell his mother? Perhaps you should take care of this one, Henrik. We could wait for something less . . . ravenous to come along?'

'Bah!' the Guardian exclaimed. I heard him stomp across the cabin. 'You want the village protected? Then I need to train the boy, and that means battling monsters—whatever monsters happen to turn up. Even these.'

This didn't exactly fill me with confidence. But I took a deep breath, reminding myself that this was my duty now, and I pushed my way inside.

'Leo!' Gilda exclaimed. 'That was quick.'

Henrik was at his desk, standing with his back to the door. He didn't look round.

'I've been hearing all about your training,' said Gilda, looking flustered at my sudden appearance. 'Henrik says you're making excellent progress.'

She patted me on the shoulder and I gave her a blank, unimpressed look.

'Just hoping not to get eaten,' I said.

Gilda laughed awkwardly. She

glanced in Henrik's direction but got no

response.

'Well, I must be going,' she said. 'The village council is meeting today.'

At the door she turned and gave me a serious look.

'Be careful, Leo,' she told me. 'And do your best. We're all depending on you.'

And with those encouraging words, she was gone.

Only now did Henrik turn to face me, moving round to the far side of his desk.

'Come here, lad,' he said. 'Tell me what you see.'

The Map of Monsters lay open on the desk and its many-coloured lights danced across the Guardian's face. I walked over, feeling the pressure of his

25

expectations. But I also felt the special thrill that only the map could bring. It was fully open, the whole of the forest spread out before me and alive with light: north to the towering mountains and west to the White River and beyond. All across the map the coloured lights showed the movements of the forest's monsters. There were great gatherings and smaller groups, pairs of monsters and many that crept through the forest alone.

'Well?' said Henrik, nodding towards the map. 'What do you think?'

I pointed to an area north-east of the village, where the White River ran alongside a range of craggy hills.

'Here,' I said. 'These blue lights must be river monsters. Most of them are keeping close to the river, but these two have strayed from the pack. They've virtually crossed over the Knucklebone Hills and they're moving about quite a lot.'

I looked up and the Guardian nodded.

'Spitfangs,' he said. 'Amphibious lizards. They usually keep to the river banks, but these two have strayed further south. I wasn't worried until today, when they started acting strangely, running about and getting far too close to the village. I don't know what's got into them, but we've got to make sure they don't get any closer.'

'We?' I said, hoping I wouldn't be out there on my own.

Henrik laughed, although it was more like a growling sort of cough.

'You, lad. I mean you,' he said. 'My leg's healed all right, but I'm too old to be chasing monsters around the forest. I've got more battle scars than a whole army put together, and my bones are creaking worse than this old cabin.'

He reached behind him and produced the pouch of stones and the slingshot. Each stone had its own special power. They could scare a monster away with a loud noise or a terrible smell, or even make them fall asleep.

'Your aim's improving,' he said. 'More or less. Just try not to waste so many stones this time. They're not easy to come by.'

I nodded and took the pouch, nerves fluttering round my stomach.

'Good,' said Henrik, folding up the Map of Monsters. 'One thing you should know about these Spitfangs,' he said. 'First they spit, then they bite. If you see their throats swell up . . . well, then you're in real trouble. Whatever you do, boy, don't get spat on. All right?'

I took the map and tucked it into my belt alongside the pouch and the slingshot.

'I'll try not to,' I said, wondering if I'd ever get any useful advice out of the old man.

TWO

I left through the back door of the
cabin, heading east along a path lined
with soft green ferns. Up above, the
treetops wrestled with the wind, but it
was strangely calm on the forest floor. I
walked quickly, Gilda's concerns echoing
in my mind: what if he gets eaten? she'd
said. And now getting eaten was all I
could think about.

This was not a false alarm, and it wasn't a test either. It was the real thing. A pair of spitting, biting lizard monsters were on a collision course with the village and it was up to me to stop them. Henrik had finally admitted that my slingshot aim was improving. Hopefully, it had improved enough to keep the Spitfangs away from the village and keep me in one piece.

The path took me over a small stream overhung by tall, crooked trees. Then it curved north, the forested ground rising steeply ahead. I figured this would be a good time to stop and consult the map.

The pair of Spitfangs had split up. One blue dot was totally still, near the southern edge of the Knucklebone Hills. The other seemed to be moving around in circles, close to a large cliff somewhere to the west of where I was standing. I checked my slingshot and the pouch of stones. I knew more about the stones now, their different powers and how to tell them apart by their symbols. But I still felt nervous and unready.

I examined the map, concentrating hard as I tried to figure out the best way to intercept the giant lizards. I was so deep in thought, in fact, that I totally missed the bright amber dot that was rushing across the map.

Wings suddenly beat around my head and paws gripped my shoulder. I spun around with a muffled cry.

Then the wings rose up and a furry, weasel-like face was hovering in front of me.

'Leo Wilder!' Starla cried out.

'I knew it was you!' she said, flapping her big, leathery wings to stay level with me. 'As soon as you got away from the village, I knew it. I sensed you inside my head, Leo Wilder. Because we are friends! Welcome back to the forest!'

Starla didn't speak with her mouth in the normal way. Instead, her voice appeared directly inside my head, a shrill, echoing sound that I was still getting used to.

'Thank you,' I replied, realizing I had a huge grin on my face. 'Where have you been? I looked for you when I was doing slingshot practice with Henrik.'

'Hmm,' said Starla, growing serious.

'I was not always on the map. Not always in the forest. But don't worry,' she said, brightening. 'I always know when Leo Wilder is here! I will always come to help you!'

'That's lucky,' I said. 'I could do with some help.'

I explained about the Spitfangs and showed Starla the map.

'Yes,' she said. 'These are a strange kind of river monster. Very quiet most of the time, but sometimes very dangerous. They move fast, Leo Wilder, and their spit is . . . Well, make sure you don't . . .'

'I know,' I interrupted. 'Don't get spat on. Believe me, I'm not planning on it.'

We moved off, following the path as it ascended through the trees. Evergreens began to appear, bringing with them a delicious pine needle smell. Starla flew on ahead, reporting back regularly, and I kept the map open, watching with increasing unease as the lights of the Spitfangs drew nearer.

I'd decided to approach the closest lizard first, the one that was currently darting about near the clifftop to the west. Somehow, I needed to convince both of these monsters to return to their proper home along the White River. There had to be a reason why they'd strayed so far from their normal habitat. Maybe they were lost and I could scare them away with one of my stones? I was trying to decide which stone would be best when Starla appeared, scampering on the forest floor with her wings folded across her back.

'Shh, Leo Wilder. Stop!' she warned me.

'Is it them?' I whispered, crouching beside a tree.

'Not monsters,' Starla said. 'Forest people.'

I frowned at her.

'What do you mean?'

'Look and see,' she replied, nodding in the direction she'd just come from.

I crept around the tree trunk, staying low. My heart beat fast. If Starla was afraid of these forest people, then they had to be bad.

I rose slowly, peering out between the trees. Then I saw what Starla was talking about.

A girl was stepping carefully through the foliage. She was about my age, but she was unlike anyone I'd ever seen before. Her clothes were dyed in many different shades of green, so that when she stopped, she blended in with the forest around her. Her boots looked soft and thin, making virtually no sound as she walked. She carried a woven basket in the crook of her arm and seemed to be looking for something, scanning the surrounding trees with a stern expression on her face. Every now and then she glanced down at the forest floor and stooped to gather something into her basket.

When she turned away from me I saw
a very sharp-looking spear strapped
across her back.

I couldn't quite believe what I was
seeing. This girl definitely wasn't from
the village. But if that was true, then
where was she from? Out here in the
forest?

A few seconds later another girl
emerged from the pine trees higher up
the hillside. She was dressed in a similar
way, and also carried a basket, but she
was younger. She was smiling excitedly
and making much more noise than the
older girl.

'Eve! Eve!' she called. 'I found twenty-three more mushrooms, and you'll never guess what else . . .'

'Willow!' the older girl scolded. 'What have I told you about wandering off? You stay where I can see or hear you. The forest is dangerous. You know that.'

The younger girl, Willow, frowned and hung her head.

I suddenly felt guilty for spying on them.

'Be careful, Leo Wilder,' said Starla, appearing beside me. 'These people are not good ones. Not good at all.'

'What do you mean?' I whispered. And immediately the two girls froze, turning to face me.

Eve stepped in front of
Willow with a protective arm
held out behind her. She put

her basket down and reached for her spear, staring intensely into the group of trees I was hiding in.

I stayed as still as I could.

The tip of Eve's spear gleamed as she took a step forwards, and I didn't like the look of it at all. I didn't like the hard expression on her face either. Holding my breath, I watched as she scanned the undergrowth around me. Willow peered out nervously from behind her, and It seemed like a long time before Eve finally lowered her spear and picked up her basket.

As they both turned to leave I breathed out quietly in relief. Then I

remembered the Spitfangs. I had to
warn them.

I hesitated for a moment, then began
to rise.

'Oh, no,' said Starla. 'Don't let them
see you!'

'Hi,' I said, stepping out from behind

the tree. 'I'm Leo.'

Eve spun to face me, narrowing her eyes. She kept her spear low by her side, but I could tell she was ready to use it.

'Who are you?' she demanded. 'What do you want?'

'I'm from the village,' I replied, beginning to regret my decision to stand up. 'We're on the trail of a pair of Spitfang Lizards. They've strayed from their territory by the White River.'

'Hmm,' Eve murmured, weighing me up with a stern look. I could tell she was as surprised to see me as I was to see her.

'My sister can fight off a Spitfang,' Willow said. 'Easy.'

'Quiet, Willow' Eve said, shushing her sister.

'Are you a hunter?' she asked me, glancing at the map in my hand. I noticed her grip tighten on her spear.

'Don't tell her anything,' Starla said, still hidden in the trees. 'These forest people are not to be trusted.'

'I'm a Guardian,' I said, ignoring Starla. 'I don't hunt the monsters. I just try to keep them and my village safe.'

Eve studied me for a moment more, then she knelt and picked up her basket, not taking her eyes off me.

'You should go back to your village,' she told me. 'It's not safe for you here.'

I wasn't sure if she meant it kindly or as some kind of threat, but before I could respond she'd turned her back on me, ushering her sister away.

'Come on, Willow,' she said. 'Let's go and find some cliff-berries.'

I watched them move off silently in the direction of the craggy rock face to the west.

'Be careful,' I called after them. 'One of the Spitfangs is near here, down by the clifftop.'

'We can look after ourselves,' came the blunt reply. 'Go home!'

A few moments later the girls were gone amongst the trees.

'I told you,' Starla said, finally emerging from behind the tree. 'Very weird people. I met some before, Leo Wilder. Not friendly. Not friendly at all.'

I nodded, still amazed that there were people living out in the forest. But then, I'd had no idea about the monsters until my Assignment had begun, so what did I know?

'We should keep going,' I said, lifting the map, but still staring into the trees after Willow and Eve.

THREE

We left the path and headed downhill, hoping to intercept the moving blue light on the map. I waded through ferns and pushed scratchy, low-hanging pine branches out of my way, while Starla flew happily through the treetops.

'Be careful, Leo Wilder,' she called down to me. 'When we find the spitting lizard thing, you should definitely not get close.'

'I won't,' I called back, my boots crunching into the slippery carpet of pine needles. 'Or maybe I will,' I said, getting tired of being treated as if I didn't know what I was doing. 'Maybe I'll give it a nice warm hug and a pat on the head.'

'Oh, no, Leo Wilder! Don't do that!'

'Or maybe I'll give the Spitfang a kiss? A nice big kiss on the snout . . .'

I was descending a steep section of the hillside, and as I spoke my feet suddenly flew out from under me and I crashed onto my behind, sliding down the slope towards a wide, dry gulley.

I landed with a thump and lay on my back feeling stunned.

I could hear Starla
flapping about, trying
to find me, but when I sat up, it wasn't
Starla I saw.

Two yellow-green, reptilian eyes peered down at me, unblinking, from about three paces away. The creature that the eyes belonged to was scaly and spiky and somewhere between a goat and a horse in size. Its scales were a mix of blues and greens and its muscular legs jutted out from the sides of its body, tapering down to viciously clawed, three-toed feet. Its head was long and snouty, with a loose flap of pinkish skin under its chin. This was the Spitfang Lizard I'd been searching for.

The monster was also utterly still. So still that it didn't even seem to be breathing.

As I lay there staring, a hopeful thought crossed my mind: maybe it was asleep?

My uncle Silas slept with his eyes open
sometimes . . .

Then the Spitfang opened its mouth
and hissed, revealing two rows of
glistening, needle-sharp teeth.

No. It definitely wasn't sleeping.

I scrambled backwards, desperately trying to climb to my feet, but the loose leaves and pine needles kept making me slip.

The Spitfang hissed at me again, its teeth dripping with saliva. The flap of skin beneath its throat pulsated, then swelled rapidly until there was a huge, bloated pouch beneath its scaly chin.

I clambered to my feet and reached for the slingshot at my belt. The lizard hissed and twitched. Its huge claws dug deeper into the ground. I knew it was about to spit.

I needed a stone, something that

would scare it off. But every time I moved my hand, the creature jerked its head and edged forwards threateningly. These monsters were fast, Starla had said. It would probably be on me before I could even load the stone, let alone fire it.

The Spitfang snapped its jaw. Its throat pouch looked like it was ready to burst.

I decided I'd have to move carefully. If this Spitfang was anything like the other lizard monsters I'd read about, then slow movements were the only way to escape attack.

Very slowly, I lifted my right foot from the ground and took a tiny step back. The lizard didn't move. That was good. I lifted my left foot, ever so slowly, hardly daring to breathe, my heart pounding like a blacksmith's hammer.

Again, the monster stayed where it was. It wanted me gone, I realized. That was all. It didn't want to fight.

I raised my right foot once again, placing it very carefully behind me, keeping my eyes on the monster, watching as its eyes twitched and it tasted the air with a long pink tongue.

It was OK. I was going to back away and everything would be fine.

Then, with the worst timing possible, Starla came crashing through the branches above.

'I'm here, Leo Wilder! I'm here! Are you all right?'

The lizard reared onto its hind legs, spooked by all the noise, and sent a gurgling stream of thick, yellow spit directly at me. I turned my back and dived to the side, but not quickly enough.

The spit hit my legs and knocked me sideways, sending me crashing awkwardly onto my side.

I tried to get up and run, but my legs wouldn't move. When I looked down I saw that they were stuck inside a cocoon of congealing yellow gunge. It was then Henrik's advice rang out in my head: first they spit, then they bite.

I turned to see the Spitfang advancing on me slowly, its teeth bared and its front claws scraping at the ground.

'Watch out, Leo Wilder!' Starla cried.

I dragged myself backwards, desperately trying to unstick my legs, but it was no use. The spit had set like glue.

Starla swooped down and hovered between me and the monster. She made an angry, high-pitched snarling noise and the lizard paused for a moment, looking puzzled. Then it continued its advance.

'Shoot a stone!' Starla cried. 'Shoot a stone!'

'I'm trying!' I said. 'I can't get them free.'

The spit had glued the pouch to my leg. I tried to open it, but my hand just stuck to the fabric. There was no way I could get at the stones.

I looked up. The lizard was almost on us.

Then a strange, gurgling, screech rang out in the distance and the Spitfang stopped in its tracks, rose onto its hind legs and faced uphill.

It shrieked in reply, a horrible, wet, throaty noise that hurt my ears and made Starla wrap her wings around her head.

A second later the lizard was gone, disappearing at lightning speed into the undergrowth, leaving the ferns thrashing behind.

I stared at where the Spitfang had been then I collapsed onto my back, breathing hard with relief.

Starla collapsed beside me.

'Now that was a close one, Leo Wilder.'

FOUR

'This stuff does not taste delicious,' said Starla, chewing at the dried Spitfang spit that covered my legs. 'In fact, Leo Wilder, it is totally disgusting.'

She tore off another strip with her sharp little teeth and spat it onto the ground.

I could almost move both legs now, and Starla had managed to free the slingshot and pouch. Sadly, it looked as if my best pair of trousers were ruined.

'Thanks,' I said, as Starla ripped away another big chunk of congealed spit. 'I think I can walk now.'

I stood up, while Starla shivered and wiped at her tongue with one of her paws. I was tempted to mention that it had only happened because she'd come charging in so noisily. But, she'd been so brave trying to defend me from the Spitfang, I decided to keep my mouth shut.

We set off, climbing the wooded hillside, aiming to rejoin the path we'd been following earlier. According to the map, the lizard whose spit I was wearing had joined its friend up on the hilltop.

'That's probably what all the shrieking was about,' I said to Starla.

'Probably,' she replied, flying through the trees not far above my head. 'These Spitfangs are really weird.'

As we climbed, the pine trees grew thinner and further apart, with boulders of all sizes scattered in between them. Then the trees disappeared completely and a huge mound of bare rock appeared before us.

This was the summit, and as we skirted around the rocks, the rest of the Knucklebone Hills slowly came into view. They rose proudly from the forest, each one capped with its own unique jumble of rocks. I paused for a moment, taking in the vastness of the forest around me and the imposing outline of the hills. I realized, once again, how little I'd experienced of the world outside the village.

From the map I knew that somewhere beyond the last of hills, the powerful White River rushed through a deeply carved ravine. This was where the Spitfangs had come from, and on the map, the hillsides nearest the river were alive with moving blue lights. That's where all the sensible lizards stayed.

But not our two.

'They're close,' I said to Starla, studying the map and trying to figure out exactly how close.

'Yes,' said Starla, hovering high above my head. 'I can see them, Leo Wilder.'

Starla led the way, further around the rocky summit, and soon I began to hear the kind of angry lizard noises that made my stomach flutter with nerves.

'They're fighting,' Starla called to me.

And as I reached a low ledge of rock and looked down, I saw that she was right.

A short way down the hillside there was a curved patch of grass. Here, the two Spitfangs lunged back and forth at each other, whipping their tails, hissing furiously and swiping with their clawed feet. I recognized the one that had attacked me by its blue and green scales. It was a big lizard, and it was frightening to see it fighting so viciously. But the second Spitfang was even bigger. It had orange and red scales that rippled as it charged about. Beneath the warring lizards I saw a small mound of bare dirt that was topped with a circle of rocks.

'That looks like a nest,' said Starla. 'A strange place to fight, Leo Wilder.'

'Maybe they both want to use it?' I suggested. 'According to Henrik's books, lizard monsters often fight over the best nesting sites.'

Starla gave me a surprised look. She didn't know I'd been reading up on monster behaviour.

But I fixed my attention on the Spitfangs. It looked like a pretty serious disagreement and I didn't really want to get involved, but the lizards were too close to the village. Looking back the way we'd come, I could see the Village Wall and I knew these monsters were fast enough to cover that distance in no time at all.

I crouched down on the ledge and drew my slingshot.

As well as my 'very slight improvement' with the slingshot, my three weeks of training and study meant I could now select the stone I actually wanted.

Starla flapped down to join me.

'We need to get them to leave the area,' I said. 'Shift them back to the far side of the hills, near the river.'

I scanned the instructions in the pouch while Starla sniffed at the stones. I don't know how, but she could smell what each of them did.

'Nothing that'll hurt them,' I said. 'We just want to scare them away.'

Starla nodded.

'Spook-stone?' I said, picking one out. It was supposed to create a dense, eerie fog, complete with shadowy floating figures. 'That could get rid of them?'

'Hmm.' Starla thought about it. 'Pretty scary for you, Leo Wilder, but I think these Spitfangs will not be afraid of some floating nonsense.'

She dug her snout into the pouch and dropped a stone into my lap.

'A screech-stone?' I said.

'A lizard hates loud noises,' said Starla. 'Everyone knows that, Leo Wilder.'

'Right,' I said, feeling slightly doubtful. But I loaded it onto the sling anyway.

'You'd better be right,' I said. 'Henrik won't like it if I waste any more stones.'

'That miserable guts doesn't like anything,' Starla replied.

She had a point.

I knelt at the edge of the rock ledge, pulled back the sling and took aim. Down below, the Spitfangs faced off against each other, thrashing their tails and hissing. Hopefully, if I landed the stone on the near side of them, the screeching noise would drive them directly away from me and away from the village—back towards the White River.

I narrowed my eyes and aligned my outstretched arm with the target, just like Henrik had taught me. I visualized the journey of the stone, visualized it landing exactly where I wanted it.

Then I sent it flying.

The screech-stone arced through the air, straight and fast. I smiled to myself. This was a good shot.

But the stone kept going.

And kept going.

And kept going.

Over the lizards and further still, landing in a thick patch of grass with a fizzing, crackling thump.

'Whoops,' said Starla.

I was about to respond when the screeching started.

It was horrible, the kind of sound a thousand baby goats might make if they all woke from the same terrible nightmare at the same time. And it was loud, so loud that it physically hurt my ears.

I clamped my hands to the sides of my head and watched as the Spitfangs fled from the noise in a state of panic. One of them ran straight up the hillside, disappearing behind the rocky summit. The other ran directly away from the sound, downhill and to the west, moving at incredible speed towards the cliff I'd seen on the map.

Starla's voice echoed in my head, barely audible with the screech-stone still howling.

'The village!' she was saying. 'It's going towards the village!'

A sickening feeling gripped me as I realized what else the Spitfang was heading for.

'Eve and Willow,' I muttered.

Starla frowned, unable to hear me.

'THE GIRLS!' I shouted, just as the screech-stone fell silent. 'They were heading the same way! Towards the clifftop!'

I stuffed the pouch back into my belt and I ran.

FIVE

I launched myself down the hillside at full speed, crashing through bushes and weaving clumsily round the trunks of the pine trees.

Starla glided through the air above me.

'Leo Wilder!' she cried. 'Look out!'

A huge fallen branch lay directly across my path, and I had just enough time to hurl myself into the air.

Somehow, I cleared the log, but I landed on one foot and totally out of control.

Starla swooped past me.

'Careful, Leo Wilder. Slow down!'

But I couldn't slow down and I didn't want to. The screech-stone I'd fired had sent the Spitfang straight towards Eve and Willow, and towards the village. If the lizard hurt them, it would be all my fault.

So I kept going, half running and half falling, faster and faster down the hillside.

I could hear the girls now: Willow's high-pitched wail and Eve's fearsome shouting. I could also hear the unmistakeable hiss of the Spitfang.

'That way!' Starla cried.

I swerved to the right, skidded down a steep, treeless bank and found myself stumbling across a small patch of level ground that ended in a line of crooked trees. Before I could even think about trying to stop, the trees were right in front of me.

It was then I noticed that beyond the trees the ground seemed to disappear completely.

I was running towards the cliff edge.

'Stop, Leo Wilder!' cried Starla.

'I can't!' I shouted back.

Then I felt her paws digging into my shoulder.

She was trying to lift me. 'Too heavy,

Leo Wilder! Too much eating!'

I ignored Starla's rude comment and leaped for a low branch in the tree directly ahead.

My fingers touched bark and I grabbed the branch as tightly as I could, my legs swinging out from under me. At my shoulder, Starla gripped harder, her wings beating furiously.

'I've got you, Leo Wilder. I've got you!'

Glancing down, I saw a drop that made my stomach lurch. A rain of pine needles fluttered out over the cliff, down and down towards distant treetops. I closed my eyes as my bodyweight swung me further out, the rough bark scratching at my palms.

Then the swing took me back towards
the cliff. I opened my eyes and at the

furthest point I let go and dropped onto the clifftop with a grunt. Only then did Starla let go of my shoulders.

'You're safe now, Leo Wilder,' she said.

'Thanks,' I replied, flat on my back and breathing hard.

Then from somewhere along the clifftop I heard Willow scream.

'Come on,' I said to Starla, dragging myself up and drawing my slingshot as I ran.

A broad, rock strewn path ran along the top of the cliff, curving around the hillside. As I ran, the sounds of trouble grew louder: shouts and cries, stamping feet, the wet, throaty hiss of the Spitfang.

Then I rounded a corner and found a desperate confrontation in progress.

With their backs dangerously close to the clifftop, the two girls stood facing the lizard. Eve was shielding Willow with her body. She'd drawn her spear and was jabbing it towards the lizard, trying to keep it away.

The creature hissed and whipped its tail. It darted from side to side, easily dodging Eve's spear. It looked angry, and all of its anger was directed at the girls.

'Get lost!' Eve shouted at the monster.

'Go on. Go!'

She took another swipe with her spear and the lizard reared up onto its hind legs, letting out a hideous, gargling shriek. The pouch beneath its chin began to swell.

'Look out!' I shouted. 'It's going to spit!'

Eve glanced over, noticing me and Starla for the first time.

'I know what Spitfangs do,' she snapped.

But I could see the fear behind her glare.

'Ungrateful,' muttered Starla, hovering at my shoulder. 'Typical forest peoples.'

'Just help me find a stone,' I said, rummaging through the pouch.

When I glanced up, I saw that the lizard's throat was bloated and pink. It could spit at any moment and I knew the spit would be strong enough to knock the girls off their feet and over the cliff. There was no time for wasting stones. I had to get this right first time.

By my side, Starla was sniffing at the pouch.

'A vine-stone!' I said, suddenly sure of what I needed. 'Can you find a vine-stone?'

'Yes, Leo Wilder, yes,' Starla replied.

An instant later she was dropping one into my hand.

I loaded the sling and looked up. The Spitfang was on its hind legs, head drawn back and ready to spit. I didn't have time to aim, didn't have time to think. Instead I let my instincts take over, raised my arm towards the monster and let the vine-stone fly.

It struck the lizard just above its forelegs, sticking to its scales with a heavy squelching sound. The lizard jerked around to face me, then twisted its neck, trying to scrape the stone away with its teeth.

But it couldn't reach, and the vines had already begun to grow.

Thin, green tendrils sprouted from the stone, rapidly growing in all directions. In a matter of seconds, the creature's body and legs were encased in a dense weave of finger-thick vines. It fell onto its side and thrashed its tail until the vines gradually covered that part of it,

too. Soon only the lizard's head was
left free. Its spit-pouch was completely
deflated and it lay on its side, glaring at
me with its huge yellow eyes.

SIX

The Spitfang strained against the vines, twisting its body and doing its best to flex its thick, muscular limbs. It snorted and hissed and the vines creaked in a way that made me slightly nervous. I'd loaded a screech-stone into my slingshot, holding it aimed and ready. Another vine-stone would have been better, but there weren't any more in the pouch.

'I don't know how long they're going to hold,' I said to Starla, who was flapping back and forth in agitation above my head.

'Not too long,' she said. 'Not long at all.'

The lizard lay still for a moment, watching me intently as if it couldn't quite believe what I'd done to it. Then it shrieked and started thrashing about on the ground. I jumped back, startled, and noticed that the girls had begun to leave, and that the lizard's yellow-eyed gaze was fixed furiously on them.

As Eve took Willow by the hand and

led her away from the cliff edge, the lizard let out a long, pitiful whine.

It followed them with its eyes, twisting its neck and continuing to whine desperately.

'I don't understand,' I said to Starla, while keeping my slingshot aimed at the monster. 'Why is it so angry with them?'

'I told you a million times,' she said. 'No one likes forest people. Not even monsters.'

I shook my head. That couldn't be it.

Then I saw Willow clutch her basket close to her chest and an idea began to form in my head.

I looked up at Starla.

'The nest!' I said. 'Up on the hill.'

Starla looked puzzled for an instant then her eyes widened.

'Yes, Leo Wilder!' she said.

Together we turned back to the girls.

They were heading into the trees, leaving the Spitfang writhing in its prison of vines.

'Wait!' I called, lowering my slingshot. 'Willow! Can I look in your basket?'

Willow turned, freezing in her tracks.

Eve glared at me.

'Ignore him, Willow,' she said. 'Come on. Let's go.'

She tugged on Willow's arm.

'Don't you want to know why that monster's so interested in you?' I asked.

'It's a lizard,' Eve said. 'Lizards are weird.'

'Especially when you steal their eggs,' I said.

Eve narrowed her eyes.

'What are you trying to say?'

I shrugged.

'Why don't you look in the basket?' I suggested, meeting her hard look with a pretty decent one of my own. Behind me, the vines creaked and stretched as the Spitfang struggled to break free.

Eve shook her head.

'Go back to your precious village,' she said. 'I think it's missing its idiot.'

'Fine,' I said. 'But those vines won't last forever. And there's another very large Spitfang out there. I imagine they'll both be wanting their eggs back.'

I watched as Willow's eyes grew wider and wider. She stared from me to the vine-entangled monster, then she held her basket out to her sister.

'I'm sorry!' Willow cried. 'They were so big and shiny and everyone at home's so hungry at the moment . . .'

'What did you do?' Eve demanded.

She grabbed Willow's basket and threw off the cover revealing the curved tops of three huge eggs.

'You know never to take an egg from a nest!' Eve scolded her sister. 'Especially from a monster's nest!'

Willow's face crumpled and she began to cry.

Beside her, Eve sighed, shook her head then gathered her sister into a quick tight hug.

'I'm sorry I shouted,' she said, stepping back and wiping the tears from her sister's cheeks, 'but the rules we have keep us safe. Do you understand now?'

'Yes,' Willow replied, sheepishly. 'I'm sorry.'

'We can take the eggs back,' I offered.

'We know where the nest is.'

Eve glanced across at me, and for the first time it was without her usual scowl.

'No,' she said. 'This is our problem, so we should put it right.'

SEVEN

Willow led the way, taking us uphill on a path I would never have seen on my own. She seemed determined to make up for her mistake with the eggs, setting such a furious pace that I struggled to keep up. I glanced back over my shoulder every few steps and gripped the slingshot in my hand, ready in case the Spitfang broke free from the vines.

Between me and Willow strode Eve, carrying the basket of lizard eggs as well as her own basket. Her spear was tied to her back and her boots made no sound at all as she wound her way up the hillside.

I peered into the treetops and caught sight of Starla as she flitted in and out of view, keeping her distance from the two sisters. I knew Eve was unfriendly, but Starla's attitude to the sisters didn't make a lot of sense to me. They actually seemed quite normal considering that they lived out here in the forest with the monsters.

We'd left the Spitfang on the clifftop, and I kept wondering how long the vines would last. As I walked, I couldn't help but imagine them snapping and the huge lizard tearing after us through the forest. I slowed down and took the map out, pausing for breath at the same time. The blue light by the cliff wasn't moving, which meant the Spitfang hadn't broken free just yet.

But the relief I felt didn't last very long. The other blue light was moving, and it was moving fast, heading towards us from the other side of the hill.

'Uh-oh,' I muttered, wondering how many of Henrik's precious stones I had left, then wondering what he'd say if I used up a whole pouch-full in one day. I quickened my pace, scrambling up the path in an attempt to catch up with the girls.

With a chaotic flap of wings, Starla appeared, hovering uncomfortably close to my face.

'One large lizard on its way!' she exclaimed. 'And it does not look totally happy, Leo Wilder.'

'Thanks,' I replied, ducking past her so I could continue my uphill scramble. 'How far are we from the nest? We have to put those eggs back before it finds us.'

She swept past me, flitting back and forth across the path.

'Maybe we make it, maybe we don't,' she replied. 'Can't you make those legs go faster, Leo Wilder?'

'I'm trying,' I puffed, my boots constantly sliding on the loose layer of pines needles. 'Hey!' I shouted to the girls. 'We need to get those eggs back fast! The other Spitfang's on its way!'

Eve paused for a moment, staring back at me with a troubled look in her eyes.

'Willow! Climb the nearest tree you can find. Do it now!' Eve yelled urgently.

Then she sprinted up the slope as if it were no slope at all, the basket of lizard eggs swinging by her side.

Willow ran for a nearby tree and scrambled up into the branches, vanishing from sight.

I stared for a moment, amazed at how fast Eve and Willow could move, then I set off running as hard as I could.

'Starla!' I shouted. 'Which way to the nest!'

She swooped down in front of me.

'Follow me, Leo Wilder! I'll get you there!'

We swerved left past a moss-covered

rock, then right along a bank of bright
yellow flowers. I had the slingshot ready
in one hand and the map gripped tight
in the other. Glancing down at the map,
my heart sank. The blue light by the cliff
was on the move, too.

'The vines have broken!' I called to
Starla. 'The other one's free!'

'That is bad, bad, bad, Leo Wilder.'
she cried. 'But we are almost there!
Follow me!'

Together, we burst through a
bristling curtain of pine branches
and emerged onto the curved, grassy
clearing just below the summit. In the
centre of the clearing Eve crouched

beside the circle of stones that marked the Spitfangs' nest. All three eggs were back in the nest.

The eggs were the Spitfangs' children, so I understood why there were so angry with us. I thought of how the lizards had been fighting over the empty nest and realised that they must have been angry with each other, too.

'Get out of here.' Eve hissed at me.

And then I saw, in the tree line just beyond her, the huge red and orange Spitfang with its teeth bared and the pouch beneath its throat already beginning to swell.

I grabbed a handful of stones from my pouch and held them out to Starla.

'Which one?' I asked, unable to take my eyes from the rapidly expanding throat of the Spitfang. It was about to spit and its long teeth dripped hungrily with saliva.

Starla sniffed at the stones in my palm.

'These are not the best stones,' she said. 'Another vine-stone would be good, or a lightning-stone, or maybe . . .'

'We don't have time for this,' I said,

stepping forward and slotting a random stone into the sling. The lizard hissed at me, then turned its attention back to Eve.

'I said, go!' she shouted. 'You're just making things worse!'

She carefully reached back for her spear, and I pulled my sling back and took aim.

Then the trees behind me shook and the second Spitfang crashed into the clearing.

I spun around and aimed my slingshot, retreating until I stood back-to-back with Eve beside the nest of shining eggs. We were surrounded. Even if I hit one of the lizards with my stone, the other one would spit and we'd be stuck, at the mercy of its slavering jaws.

'Well, this is great,' Eve said. 'What do we do now, Mr Guardian?'

The lizard in front of her hissed and I could hear the throaty sound of its spit getting ready to fly. I may have been imagining things, but the other Spitfang, the one I'd trapped in the vines, looked particularly pleased to be getting its revenge. I prepared to fire, hoping I hadn't chosen a stink-stone. Then Starla called out to me:

'Just walk away!' she said

'If we move, they'll spit!' I replied.

'All they want is their eggs, Leo Wilder! Trust me! You have to walk away now!'

I stared into the angry yellow eyes

of the Spitfang facing me, wondering if Starla could be right. The fact was, I didn't have any better ideas.

'I'm going to walk away from the nest,' I said to Eve. 'Really slowly. You want to join me?'

The lizard facing Eve hissed and gargled, ready to spit.

'Why not?' Eve replied.

And together, ever so slowly, we began edging away.

As soon as I moved, the Spitfang closest to me reared up and hissed, its mouth so wide I saw half way down its throat. I kept moving away, expecting the spit to engulf me at any moment.

But the further away we got from the
nest, the less aggressive the lizards became.
They watched us all the way, but their throat
pouches slowly deflated and their razor-
toothed mouths gradually swung shut.

Then, once we'd crept about ten paces

away, the pair of Spitfangs rushed in to nuzzle at their precious eggs, making a rough, throaty noise that sounded almost like purring.

Eve and I stood there for a moment, watching as the fearsome monsters gently curled their long scaly bodies around the eggs and continued to purr.

I felt the breeze from Starla's wings on my cheek.

'You were right,' I said as she landed on my shoulder. 'They just wanted their eggs back.'

'Of course I was right,' she replied, folding her wings away neatly. 'You should always listen to Starla.'

Always.

No exceptions.'

I turned towards Eve.

'Do you think Willow's all . . .?' I began to say.

But Eve was gone.

'Hmm,' I said. 'She could at least have said goodbye.'

'I told you, Leo Wilder. These forest people . . .'

She shook her head in disapproval.

It didn't matter. We'd returned the eggs to their parents and stopped the Spitfangs' rampage. Anyway, something told me we'd be seeing Eve and Willow again.

EIGHT

Starla and I headed back through the forest together. Evening was drawing in and the air felt cool and fresh. In the west, back towards the hills, the sky was turning pinkish orange. The forest seemed peaceful, and for the first time I thought that maybe it wouldn't be such a terrifying place to live.

Starla was quieter than usual. Perhaps

because we'd had such a busy day. Or perhaps because she hadn't enjoyed being around strangers. Either way, she flew high above me pretending to scout out a route despite the fact that we both knew exactly how to get home.

Only when we were close to the Guardian's cabin did Starla drop down and perch on my shoulder.

'You think I was mean about those forest girls,' she said.

I twisted my neck to look at her. Her amber eyes seemed sad.

'Well,' I said. 'You were a bit mean.'

Starla nodded.

'I just couldn't figure out why you were so wary of them,' I said. 'They seemed all right to me, more or less. But then, I'm a stranger in the forest, so I don't really know how things work around here.'

'Not a stranger, Leo Wilder!' Starla replied, brightening up. 'You are the new Guardian. And much, much nicer than the last one. A very grumpy person, that one.'

'Well, you're right about that,' I said.

'But really,' Starla said. 'Some forest people are not good.' She paused, growing serious again. 'When I was young and not too clever, I went exploring, away from my home place in the desert. Some of those forest people tricked me and put me in a cage. A horrible cage. When I escaped, a long time later, my family clan of Leatherwings had moved. They were nowhere, and the desert is hard to live in without your family clan. This is why I am a desert monster all alone in the forest, Leo Wilder. It's because of those people. Forest people. You are our Guardian and I trust you. But for other people? I have no trust. I know it's mean, but I can't help it.'

We walked on in silence for a while, Starla riding on my shoulder, her tiny claws gripping gently and her wing brushing against my ear.

'I'm really sorry you lost your family,' I said. 'And I understand why you don't trust people after what happened to you. Do you miss the desert?' I asked.

'Yes,' she replied. 'But I also like the forest. There are many more delicious insects. Plus, we are friends now and we chase giant lizards together!'

At that she leaped from my shoulder and flapped ahead.

'Come on, Leo Wilder. The grumpy one's cabin is here. Time to finish your day of work, yes?'

I said goodbye to Starla and stepped inside, hoping she'd be all right.

The cabin was cold and it smelled of the salted fish Henrik had obviously enjoyed for his lunch. I found him at his desk, scribbling words onto a thick piece of parchment. He didn't look up when I entered, nor did he stop scribbling, so I faked a very loud cough to get his attention.

'Well, boy?' he growled.

I told him what had happened,
leaving out the bit where I'd misfired
the screech-stone and sent one of the
Spitfangs charging towards the village.

He didn't really need to know that, and anyway, he didn't seem to be paying much attention.

Only when I finished my report did he respond, grunting in a way that was impossible to interpret.

'Those girls are trouble,' he said, laying his quill down carefully on the desk. 'Best to steer clear of them, lad. Same goes for anyone else you meet out there. So, how many stones did you waste this time?' he asked me.

'I only used two,' I said. 'One for each lizard.' Hopefully, he wouldn't ask me exactly how I'd used them, or notice the dried crust of lizard spit on my trousers.

'Hmm,' he muttered, narrowing his eyes at me. 'Well then.'

He tapped the desk with his finger, obviously keen to get back to his work.

'You can leave the equipment here,' he said.

I placed the slingshot, pouch and map on the desk, taking a sneaky look at his parchment as I did so. The title along the top read: The True Memoirs of Henrik the Red, Guardian and Protector of the Immeasurable Forest. The whole page was covered with Henrik's cramped, spidery handwriting.

'Perhaps we'll make a Guardian out of

you yet,' he said as I backed away from desk.

'Do you really think so?' I asked, a huge smile spreading across my face.

'I said might,' Henrik grumbled. 'No need to get carried away, boy. I expect you'll find some way to mess the next one up.'

He was probably right, but I refused to stop smiling until I'd left the cabin.

I arrived at the Village Wall still feeling fairly pleased with myself. I even managed to find the secret door relatively quickly, twisting the mechanism and letting myself in to the back room of the turnip man's storehouse. The man himself was fast asleep, slumped peacefully on top of a large sack of turnips with his chin on his chest. I could only conclude that working with turnips was an extremely tiring business.

The sky was growing dark and I passed windows flickering with candlelight as I wound my way through the back alleys of the village. A goat bleated loudly somewhere nearby and was answered by the barking of several dogs. All the people I passed seemed to be hurrying home for dinner, and the delicious smells drifting on the air made my stomach gurgle in anticipation.

I reached the main street that led downhill to the market and crossed over towards my house. My legs felt suddenly exhausted and heavy, the events of the day running through my mind like a particularly vivid dream.

When I pushed open the front door I found a fire crackling in the grate and the table set for four people. A clanging of pots came from the kitchen along with the rich, warm aroma of Mum's spicy vegetable stew.

'I'm home!' I shouted, expecting Mum to poke her head round the corner.

But it was Jacob who appeared from the kitchen.

'Your mum said I could stay for dinner,' he said, grinning as he wielded a large wooden spoon that was dripping broth all over the floor. 'I'm stirring things while she goes for more bread.'

'You do get through a lot of bread,' I said.

Jacob shrugged. 'I'm a growing lad,' he said. 'Plus, it takes a lot of energy working in the Records Office all day. I have to listen to Master Aldred's boring stories over and over again. It's hard work.'

We went into the kitchen and watched

the pot of stew bubbling away on the stove top, Jacob stirring it now and then. I asked him about the Records Office and whether he wanted to stay there once his Assignment was over.

'I'm not sure,' he said. 'It's nice and easy, but I don't really want to turn into Master Aldred. He's kind of boring.'

I nodded, thinking a similar thought about Henrik.

For a while, we were quiet, the only sound coming from the bubbling pot. Then Jacob looked up at me, a strange expression on his face.

'I saw you go into the woods,' he said.

My chest went cold. I opened my mouth, but couldn't think of what to say.

'I know you work outside the village,' Jacob said, 'but I watched you from the top of the Wall. You walked right into the trees and kept going. I waited for ages and you didn't come back.'

He watched me closely as he spoke, the big spoon dripping by his side.

My mind worked furiously.

What was I supposed to say? I didn't want to lie to Jacob. He was my best friend. But my whole Assignment was based on a very important lie. A lie that kept everyone in the village safe. A lie that kept the monsters safe. I couldn't tell Jacob the truth, no matter how badly I wanted to.

'I was at the turnip patch,' I said, my heart sinking as I lied. 'It's a little way into the forest but Gilda says its safe. It's the only place the turnips will grow.'

Jacob tilted his head, thinking.

'Turnips?' he repeated.

'Yeah,' I said. 'Turnips.'

He shrugged. 'Hmm. I guess I never really thought about where all those turnips came from.'

He went back to stirring the stew, peering into the pot so intently that I couldn't tell whether or not he'd believed me. Thankfully, Mum came hurrying in with two big loaves of bread under her arm.

'How's the stew going, boys?' she said, squeezing my shoulder with her free hand. 'Lulu's on her way, so let's get it on the table. Your sister always comes home hungry.'

We sat down for dinner and shared our stories of the day over the delicious stew and bread. Mum had been at the village hall, sharing her midwinter festival ideas with the council. Lulu had started work on the damaged roof of one of the grain stores. Jacob shared one of Master Aldred's more interesting stories. And I, of course, talked about turnips.

By the end of the meal Jacob seemed totally normal again, as if we'd never had our conversation in the kitchen. He helped me clear up and wash the dishes, and when he left we agreed to meet for lunch again the next day.

That evening, as I sat by the fire with

Mum and Lulu and Stickle the cat, I decided I would have to be more careful. I couldn't risk Jacob—or anyone else—finding out what I was doing in the forest.

It was a strange feeling, as if I was growing apart from the people around me, just a little, because of the lies I had to tell. But it was my responsibility now, my mission to protect the forest and all the creatures within it. I couldn't slip up. Not even once.

As the fire burned low and we all grew sleepy, I leaned back in my chair and thought of the forest and the rocky hilltops. I thought about Eve and Willow who were living out there, right now, in amongst the dark trees and all the scuttling, lurking monsters. I glanced around at Mum and Lulu and Stickle and felt very lucky and glad to have my family and the walls of my home around me.

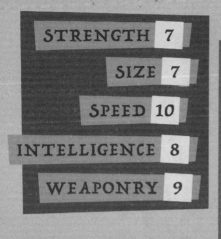

STRENGTH	7
SIZE	7
SPEED	10
INTELLIGENCE	8
WEAPONRY	9

MONSTER TYPE
River Monster

HABITAT
White River area

DIET
Fresh-water fish, small forest animals

DESCRIPTION

The second largest lizard south of the mountains, an adult Spitfang can measure up to seven paces from snout to tail-tip. Although they spend most of their time in and around the fast-flowing White River, pairs of Spitfangs climb into the Knucklebone Hills once a year to lay their eggs. Spitfangs are fiercely protective of their young and have been known to fight off much larger creatures when threatened.

ATTACK STYLE

The Spitfang hunts using its superior speed and can immobilise its prey by spitting an incredibly sticky substance produced in its throat-pouch. The Spitfang then devours its prey using its long, sharp fangs.

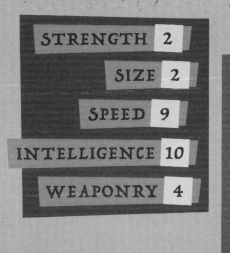

STRENGTH	2
SIZE	2
SPEED	9
INTELLIGENCE	10
WEAPONRY	4

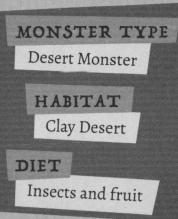

MONSTER TYPE

Desert Monster

HABITAT

Clay Desert

DIET

Insects and fruit

DESCRIPTION

The Leatherwing is a small, furry, four-legged creature that flies using its oversized, featherless wings. Leatherwings live together in large families, or 'clan-groups', travelling across the vast Clay Desert in search of seasonal feeding grounds. Leatherwing clan-groups often build temporary burrows in the walls of ravines, their sand-coloured fur providing highly efficient camouflage.

ATTACK STYLE

Though small, Leatherwings can be ferocious, and will use their sharp teeth and claws to fend off predators. Their agility in the air makes them very successful insect hunters.

ABOUT THE AUTHOR

KRIS HUMPHREY

Kris has done his fair share of interesting jobs (cinema projectionist, blood factory technician, bookseller, teacher). But he's always been writing—or at least thinking about writing.

In 2012 Kris graduated with distinction from the MA in Writing for Young People at Bath Spa University, winning the award for Most Promising Writer. He is the author of two series of books for young readers: *Guardians of the Wild* and now, *Leo's Map of Monsters*.

PETE WILLIAMSON

Pete is a London-based writer, illustrator, and animation designer, who has illustrated over 65 books including *Stitch Head* and *Skeleton Keys: The Unimaginary Friend*.

Ready for more incredible adventures? Try these!